GR1-2
9163701

J.D. AND THE GREAT BARBER BATTLE

written by
J. DILLARD

illustrated by
AKEEM S. ROBERTS

Kokila

P9-CWE-988

KOKILA
An imprint of Penguin Random House LLC, New York

First published in the United States of America by Kokila,
an imprint of Penguin Random House LLC, 2021

Text copyright © 2021 by John Dillard
Illustrations copyright © 2021 by Akeem S. Roberts

Penguin supports copyright. Copyright fuels creativity, encourages
diverse voices, promotes free speech, and creates a vibrant culture.
Thank you for buying an authorized edition of this book and for
complying with copyright laws by not reproducing, scanning,
or distributing any part of it in any form without permission.
You are supporting writers and allowing
Penguin to continue to publish books for every reader.

Kokila & colophon are registered trademarks of Penguin Random House LLC.

Visit us online at penguinrandomhouse.com.

Library of Congress Cataloging-in-Publication Data is available.

Printed in the United States of America

ISBN 9780593111543 (PBK)
1 3 5 7 9 10 8 6

ISBN 9780593111529 (HC)
1 3 5 7 9 10 8 6 4 2
FRE

Design by Jasmin Rubero | Text set in Neutraface Slab Text family

This book is a work of fiction. Any references to historical events, real people, or real places are used fictitiously. Other names, characters, places, and events are products of the author's imagination, and any resemblance to actual events or places or persons, living or dead, is entirely coincidental.

The publisher does not have any control over and does not assume any responsibility for author or third-party websites or their content.

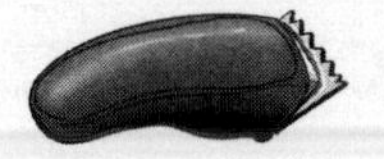

To my mother for being such a patient parent, my family for loving me for who I am, and my siblings for the memories we created over the years. To my dear friend Anje, this book wouldn't be possible without your dedication and belief in me, and for that, I thank you.

–J. Dillard

CONTENTS

CHAPTER 1

A Crooked Fade

"Sit still and look straight into the mirror," my mom said as she turned on a set of clippers.

The buzzing sound made me a little nervous. I shifted on my stool in the one bathroom my entire family of six (three adults and three kids) shared. It was the Sunday night before the start of third grade, and I was in the middle of a family tradition. In the Jones family, none of us kids got our hair cut before we turned nine. Up until now, my mom always cornrowed my hair and I'd liked it that way, but I was excited for my first real haircut.

I had been checking out my friends' haircuts all summer for ideas.

My friend Xavier, who lived across the street, had his cool dad cut his hair into the most amazing hi-top fade. But Mr. Boom was an ex-marine and strict. He made it clear HIS time and HIS money were only for HIS kids. Even when he took us all for ice cream he made sure everybody's parents gave their kids enough money to pay for our own stuff. No way I was ever asking him for anything.

"Come back with five dollars!" I imagined him saying if I asked him for a haircut.

And I'd want to yell back, "Your prices are steep!"

But not with Mr. Boom. I'd just say "Yes, sir!" to everything.

My best friend, Jordan, who lived next door, also had cool hair thanks to his older brother, Naija.

Naija had already graduated from college. He would come home after work, change into his clothes that were straight fire, and sometimes cut his and Jordan's hair. He had skills and could cut designs like playing cards into the back of his head. I would watch him and study his technique for hours. But it seemed to be happening less and less. He was a grown man with a full-time job, a new car, and a girlfriend. Naija didn't have time to cut hair all day.

I didn't just want to copy one of my friends' haircuts, though. I had so much hair that maybe I could get a small Afro with an edge up like Steph Curry. Or even something wilder like that quarterback on the Kansas City Chiefs, Patrick Mahomes.

Jordan had an iPhone and sometimes I would look on his Instagram account at barber hashtags. I loved the guy who cut designs into people's heads and then colored in the outline with a pencil.

I was good at art. I always kept a set of colored pencils and paper in my backpack so I could draw whenever I felt like it. After I saw those Instagrams, I started drawing myself with all types of Marvel characters cut into the back of my head.

Deep down, I knew I could never get The Amazing Spider-Man or any of those other styles I really liked, especially since there was only one barbershop in town, Hart and Son. They offered three types of kids' haircuts—a baldie, a Caesar, or a fade. Sometimes I'd go with my friends on Saturdays, and getting a haircut there took longer than it did to sit through one of Pastor's Sunday sermons. Your day was shot to pieces. I figured my mom could manage something simple, and plus I knew we did not have extra money to spend.

"I want a basic fade," I told my mom.

I asked for her phone and showed her a picture of Michael B. Jordan, the villain from the movie *Black Panther*.

"Okay, baby," she said. "I can't believe you are going to third grade."

I loved the weekly time my mom set aside to style my hair. My younger brother, my older sister, plus my grandparents, lived with us. It was hard to get alone time with Mom. Especially since she ALWAYS seemed to be in school, even more than me!

At first, she told us she was going back to school to become a nurse. But after spending six months working at the hospital, she quit.

"I hate the hospital," Mom said one night after a long shift. "Everybody isn't treated the same."

I didn't know exactly what happened, but I used to overhear her talking to my granddad about people being turned away for not having insurance or patients being given pills they didn't need!

So after she sat at the dinner table one night with tears in her eyes, Granddad told her if she hated the job that much, she just had to stop.

"There's plenty of other jobs in the world," he told her.

I knew it was hard for her. Mom loved medicine and her dream was to become a nurse and help sick people. It made me so proud to hear how great she was at it and how neat and clean she kept all the patients' rooms. It made me keep my bedroom extra clean, too.

So Mom went back to school to get something called an MBA and her thick books that said ANATOMY now said things like STATISTICS 101 and MANAGEMENT. She had told us she had seen a job opening in the mayor's office, but she needed this MBA thing to apply.

Mom's super smart. She didn't always get a 100 on her tests, and she didn't expect us to, but she said the important thing was to always try as hard as you could.

A couple of years ago, all of us moved in with my grandparents after my granddad had a heart attack.

"It'll just be for two months, until Granddad feels better, then we'll move back with Dad," my mom had told us.

Well, two months turned into two years.

Dad sent money sometimes, and Mom never said anything bad about him, but I didn't really know why they split up. They met when they were track stars at Mississippi Valley State, and even today Mom had what she called her "runner's legs." Sometimes she would race me and my sister around the big track at the local high school and she'd remind us why her nickname as a kid had been "Cheetah."

So it was my mom, my older sister, Vanessa, my baby brother, Justin, and my grandparents, Mr. and Mrs. Slayton Evans, all in an old house built in the 1930s. Like most houses in Meridian, Mississippi, it had a closed-in porch so you could sit outside when it was hot, which was most days, and all the rooms were on one floor. Luckily, I still got my own room since Vanessa slept with Mom and Justin loved sleeping with my grandparents.

"Baby, did you hear me?" my mom asked. I checked the time on her phone. It had been about twenty minutes already, and she'd finished cutting my hair.

"Well, what do you think?" she said. "I can't believe how grown you look."

I stared into the mirror.

What I saw was not good.

My mom had cut my hair down, all right, but my hairline looked like a hilltop or a mountain range. It definitely wasn't straight like I'd seen in pictures or on my friends.

"I can't go to school tomorrow looking like . . . this!" I told my mom.

"Nothing is wrong with your hair," she said. "You are not missing out on the first day of school. Now please get ready for bed."

I sighed and my shoulders fell three inches as I reached for my toothbrush and started to get ready to brush my teeth.

That night, I couldn't sleep.

Maybe I could fake being sick?

My hair looked terrible.

I didn't want anyone at school to see me like this.

How many ways could the third-grade class of Douglass Elementary make fun of a bad haircut?

Well, I was about to find out.

CHAPTER 2

The Nervous Breakfast

The next morning my entire family sat around eating grits, eggs, bacon, and buttered toast with jelly. Granddad had to watch his diet now, but he could never pass up a good piece of bacon or two.

My family was always busy, but Grandma loved to make everyone breakfast before we all left the house. "Fuel for the day," she'd say as she and my grandfather drank cup after cup of coffee without talking much.

The people in my family weren't big talkers except my sister, Vanessa. I was pretty sure she was friends with every girl in Meridian between the ages of ten and thirteen. The only person in my family who had a cell phone was my mother, and so Vanessa would spend as much time as she could talking on my grandparents' landline, dragging the cord around the house as she talked.

I sat at the table quieter than normal, wearing a Mississippi Bulldogs baseball cap.

"James, take that hat off while you're eating!" my granddad said.

Granddad, a tall, slim man with glasses, had recovered well from his heart attack. In fact, even though he had retired from running the local JCPenney, his health scare inspired him to go into the burial insurance business.

"We're all going to die, right?" he said. Granddad treated it like any other regular fact.

Everyone in our family had a burial insurance policy. Even us kids.

Granddad didn't play. We couldn't even say "Huh?" or "What?" around him. Everything was "Yes ma'am," "Yes sir," "No ma'am," and "No sir."

And his punishments were terrible—like not playing outside for a week or making us read boring books aloud to him and give reports.

So the first time he asked, I took off my hat.

No one said anything. They just looked at one another nervously until finally, Vanessa spoke up.

"What happened to J.D.'s braids?" she asked.

"I cut his hair. It looks fine," my mom said. "Now let's finish eating. Everybody has a long day."

The morning was moving too fast, and I'd have to leave for the bus soon. I needed to think of something quick.

"I want a ride to school today," I said.

"Why?" my mom asked. "You always take the bus with Jordan."

Granddad jumped in before I could continue.

"Stop this hardheaded act you got going on this morning, James!" my granddad said.

What he meant was that we already had our rides figured out. He took my mom to school, my grandmother and Justin to her ceramics studio, and he dropped off Vanessa on the way. Vanessa was already in middle school even though she was only in fifth grade. In Meridian, grades five through eight were all in a separate building. Her school was close to Mom's college.

"Oh, Lord! James, stop all this fighting first thing in the morning," Grandma piped in.

"Oh, Lord" was her favorite thing to say. Grandma, a deep-brown-skinned woman who kept her salt-

and-pepper hair cut short, LOVED church and she was the reason we always had to go. And not just on Sunday mornings. There was weeknight Bible study, Sunday morning Bible school, and choir. Granddad played piano at church sometimes and even practiced on the Baldwin piano in the living room. Mom and Vanessa were excellent singers. I usually lip-synched. Musical talent was something that skipped over me, but I was good at art like Grandma.

Like Granddad, Grandma didn't play, so I dropped it.

On a normal day, I loved taking the bus with Jordan. He was my best friend, but he could also give me a hard time.

Jordan would definitely have something to say about my hairline, and I would need EXTRA-tough skin to make it through the ride to school.

CHAPTER 3

The Most Horrible First Day

I snuck out of the house with my baseball cap and walked to the bus stop with my jacked-up hairline covered.

I stood quietly next to Jordan, and it wasn't long before he had something to say.

"You never wore a hat to school before, J.D.," he said as he knocked my hat to the ground, sending up a puff of red Mississippi dirt when it landed.

"Whoa!" he said as soon as he saw my head. "What happened to your hair? Your hairline looks like LeBron James's."

"My mom did it," I said. "It's okay, though. I'm going to get it fixed."

"By who? I know you don't have money to go to the barbershop. You don't even have money to pay Naija for a haircut!" Jordan said, rubbing it in.

The ride to school only got rougher when Jordan took my hat and tossed it around the bus and even more kids saw my hairline.

I pulled out my notebook and started to draw pictures of comic book characters and cartoons. I would usually draw the entire Marvel universe over and over, but today's teasing called for something more complicated, like Lego Batman.

My art was award-winning. Once I got third in a competition for a sketch of a bass fish. It was still hanging up on a wall in the Meridian mall.

"J.D.'s hair looks worse than Kevin Durant's!" Xavier said, smacking my notebook closed.

"Yeah, J.D., you looked better with your braids."

That comment came from a girl named Jessyka. Jessyka always sat with my friends and me at lunch because she was on the peewee football team with us. She wore her hair in ponytail twists, and her nails were always painted different cool colors and designs every week. Sometimes while we ate, we'd look at YouTube videos on her phone. I always wanted to watch barber channels.

Jessyka was also Vanessa's friend from kids' track-and-field. And she wasn't just ON the team, she was the STAR. Jessyka anchored the boys' and girls' 4 x 100 relay team, so that meant she was faster than EVERYBODY. She was so good, she got to run with ten- and eleven-year-olds. Sometimes she would come over to my house and paint Vanessa's nails.

"My mom wants me to look like Flo-Jo when I run my races," she told me. "Flo-Jo is my hero! I watch YouTube videos of her. I'm going to start uploading videos of my own races soon. And maybe videos of me doing other kids' nails."

I wasn't exactly sure who "Flo-Jo" was, but when

I asked my mom, she said Flo-Jo was an amazing track star and her hero, too.

Even Jessyka's last name, Fleet, made her sound like a born athlete.

It was so embarrassing to hear her say something bad about my hair.

But if I was being honest, I was used to being teased.

My clothes and shoes were hand-me-downs from my aunt and uncle in North Carolina. They had kids a bit older than me and mailed a box of my cousins' used clothes every time the weather changed, so I was always out of style.

Before, my hair was the only thing no one made fun of!

We finally pulled up to Douglass Elementary after the longest bus ride ever. Nothing had changed about it from the year before. Everything about Douglass was old. Our dusty schoolbooks nearly fell apart, the stairs creaked when you stepped on them. One time a kid almost fell through!

We had to change classes after every subject, and although I tried to keep my hat on in between, every teacher told me I had to take it off when I sat down at my desk. So all morning, different groups of kids of all ages could get a crack in.

"Yo, your hair looks a mess!"

"J.D.'s MOM cut his hair . . . !"

Jordan could always get the other kids to pipe down if it went too far. But Jordan was never in class with me because I was in honors classes. He could be, too, but I think he filled in the wrong bubbles on multiple-choice tests on purpose.

I knew I could meet up with Jordan again at lunch and maybe the lunch ladies would let me keep my hat on while I ate.

No such luck.

Because Mom was still a student, I qualified for free lunch. School didn't offer the most exciting food in the world, but since it was the first day, there was pizza and tater tots.

"J.D.! Good to see you back in school!" Ms. Carol said. She was a lunch lady with a close-cropped gray haircut. She smiled and scooped up a handful of tater tots for me. "Now take that hat off, you know it's not allowed."

Unbelievable!

As I made my way to the lunch table to sit next to Jordan, it seemed as if the whole world was slowing down and everyone was looking at my hair.

The first thing I noticed when I sat down between Jordan and Xavier was all the new Marvel character lunch boxes. The few times a year my mom packed my lunch, it was always in a brown bag.

"The food inside is the same, isn't it?" my granddad responded whenever I tried to complain.

Sitting between Jordan and Xavier, I quietly put a piece of pizza into my mouth. I wasn't in the mood to say much to anyone.

Jessyka sat across from us.

"I won my race again this weekend, J.D.," Jessyka said. "I'm going to be the best wide receiver our team has ever seen!"

"I bet you're right," I replied. "I'm still getting used to switching from offense to defense."

"Hmm. It's probably better for you not to get hit all the time," she said.

Wait, what was that supposed to mean?

Jessyka brought out the newest edition of *Spider-*

Man. Last year she was Gwen Stacy for Halloween.

She started to read the comic and then stopped, looking up at me.

"You know, J.D., you should let Xavier's dad cut your hair next time," she said. "I like how his hair looks."

Jordan and Xavier couldn't stop laughing.

If this was going to be every day of third grade, I knew I wasn't going to be able to take it.

I needed a plan, and maybe my mom's box of hair supplies could help.

CHAPTER 4
Jordan's Magical House

Like I did every day after school, I went straight to Jordan's house from the bus.

It was amazing because everything I didn't have, Jordan did!

Here's a list of everything I loved about Jordan's house:

His multiple video game consoles.

Junk food.

Cable television and central air.

No curfew.

Peace and quiet.

Best of all, Jordan came from a family of Creasters—they only went to church on Christmas and Easter—so he had plenty of free time. The only things my family allowed were school, sports, and church.

Dinner at Jordan's house was always prepared at the same time and his mom, Mrs. Mathews, who owned a cleaning business, just said, "J. D., make yourself a plate!" and let me stuff myself with macaroni and cheese and homemade cornbread. Jordan's dad, who was retired, spent most of his time at home and would eat with us, too.

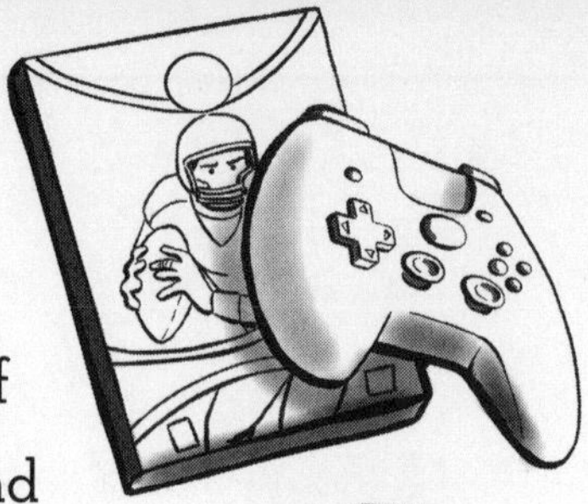

Jordan had just gotten the newest version of Madden NFL. Since we both did peewee football, we loved playing against each other, calling our own plays and fake coaching our own squads.

"Got you again," I said as my quarterback scrambled for a touchdown.

"Maybe we can start playing for money and I can save up enough to go get a haircut from Hart and Son," I joked.

I looked down at the cover of Madden NFL 20. Patrick Mahomes was on the cover. I picked up the box and slammed it against my forehead.

"If only I could get my hair to look like his!" I yelled out.

"Well, that ain't happening at Hart and Son," Jordan said. "You know they only cut Caesars, baldies, and fades. They don't even know who Patrick Mahomes is. Plus, you have to sit there all day."

Jordan was right.

There wasn't a whole lot to do in Meridian, so sometimes I tagged along with a friend who was going to the barbershop.

Hart and Son were exactly that—a father and son, Henry Sr. and Henry Jr.

Henry Sr. was a tall, skinny old man, maybe older than the Earth. Imagine a tall blade of grass with square oversized glasses, a small, neat Afro, and cargo pants held up high with a belt. That was Henry Sr.

He rarely stayed in the shop for a long time, only for a few hours in the morning to cut the hair of his grown-up clients.

Henry Jr. was in charge of keeping the shop going,

and was a lot shorter and rounder than his dad. But since there wasn't any competition in town, he could run things however he wanted, no questions asked.

There was no sign-in sheet, and make-ahead appointments were not allowed. Henry Jr. would just take a headcount and go from there—first come, first served.

A kid's haircut cost seven dollars and fifty cents. There were no pictures on the wall to choose from, and Henry Sr. definitely didn't know any famous people under the age of fifty.

"I want to look like Odell Beckham Jr.," I heard a kid say one day.

"Junior? Who the heck is Odell Beckham Jr.?" Henry Sr. said.

It was hopeless. You just had to sit, and sit, and sit, and sit for hours until it was your turn.

When you have that much time to sit, you take notice of how the Harts ran the shop—from how clean Henry Jr. kept everything to how long it took him to complete each haircut. One time I was there, I even saw salespeople come into the shop with new haircutting gadgets and styling products.

Folks felt so comfortable around the Harts that they often dropped their kids off at the shop and left while they ran errands.

I didn't know the Hart family well, but every now and then I'd see them during fellowship at church. Henry Sr. and Jr. were always getting awards for doing things like giving out free haircuts to people in need and working in soup kitchens. Henry Sr. even got something called the "trailblazer" award because he'd been cutting hair in the same spot for fifty-eight years!

"Well," Jordan said.

"Well, what?"

"Haven't you been listening?" he asked. I guess I hadn't. "Why don't you just take your mom's clippers and shave your whole head bald? It's better than what you have right now!"

I thought about what Jordan said as we finished our last game of Madden. I was so desperate, his idea didn't sound half-bad.

Well, not the bald part.

But hey, Michael Jordan was bald, and so was The Rock.

CHAPTER 5

Another Bad Hairstyle

By the next Sunday after church, I knew I had to do something. Jordan and the rest of the kids at school would never run out of cracks.

The thought of going back on Monday and taking in another week of insults made me not want to get out of bed.

I had seen my mother give herself a "relaxer" out of a box about once a month. It was a white cream that made her hair stick-straight, and she kept it short like some actress named Halle Berry.

"This hairstyle was so popular back in the day, and I liked short hair when I ran track, plus everyone said I had the right head shape for it," Mom said when I asked her why she never changed her hair.

"I guess back then I just thought it was easier.

But one of these days I'm going to stop relaxing it," she'd say. "I just don't have time right now."

Mom wasn't the best stylist. She would wash Vanessa's hair every weekend and put it into a single braid going down her neck, but Vanessa would always take it down and redo it. She would spend hours twisting her hair before taking the twists out in the morning and tying a headband around her head.

Sometimes Vanessa would stand at the mirror snipping at her hair with a pair of scissors. Her hair always looked better after she was done fussing with it.

I thought back to what Mom said about making her hair "easier" to do.

My friend Xavier's hair was kinda straight—maybe it would be easier to cut my hair into something cool if I relaxed it.

I knew my mom kept her relaxer next to the clippers under the sink in the bathroom.

So, after everyone went to sleep, I crept in there and read the box.

The instructions were followed by the words:

WARNING: Contains alkali. CAUTION: THIS PRODUCT WILL CAUSE IRRITANCY REACTION WHEN IT COMES INTO CONTACT WITH THE SKIN.

Then there were a million more long words, some I did not know, but the warning also said the product could cause blindness if it got into my eyes and that I should wear gloves when handling.

Well, I had no plan to put it in my eyes, and my mom used it in her hair.

How bad could it really be?

I followed the instructions and kept the white cream on my head for fifteen minutes and washed it out before I got into bed. That night, I thought about the warning label and all the things that could go wrong.

The results the next morning weren't, uh, exactly what I was hoping for. My hair was kinda straight, but not completely, and I had a small burn at the back of my neck. I ran a brush over it and slicked it back. I put my Bulldogs cap on before going down to the breakfast table.

Granddad didn't even have to say a thing this time. His look alone told me he wasn't pleased.

I took off my cap, and Vanessa gasped loudly.

"Did you perm your hair with mom's relaxer kit?" she asked.

"It was a mistake," I told her. "I won't use it again."

"Well, good—don't. What you did looks worse than what Mom did," Vanessa said. "Too bad it's going to take a MONTH for it to grow out."

A MONTH?

What had I done?!

»»««

The next whole week at school was even worse than the first one.

During lunch, to take my mind off my hair, I pulled out my sketchbook. I didn't even eat. I just turned my head away from my friends and put it down on the table as I completed my latest masterpiece—Thanos turning all the kids who had made fun of my hair into dust.

"You know, my parents showed me a video called 'Thriller' over the weekend," Jessyka told me as she sipped from a fruit juice box. "You look like that singer in it."

"Yeah, your head looks fried," Xavier said.

I couldn't even think of anything to say back to them, so I kept my head down and finished my drawing.

The only happy memory I had from the first two weeks of third grade was seeing Ms. Scott every morning in Reading class. She worked at a beauty counter inside JCPenney for her second job, and she looked different every day. When I used to visit my granddad at the mall before he retired, I always asked him to take me by her counter so I could get sprayed with cologne. When Ms. Scott saw how bad my hair looked, she let me keep my hat on the whole class.

The teasing continued at Bible study, at football practice, and even at home with Vanessa.

The last straw was when I was forced to sing at choir on Sunday with my head exposed, standing there looking ridiculous clapping and swaying in front of the whole congregation with my semi-straight hair.

I couldn't take it anymore.

I had to do something about my hair.

CHAPTER 6

Me vs. the Clippers

Mom prepared our post-church meal early in the morning before we left so we could eat together before we all scattered. My grandmother usually taught a private ceramics class after church on Sundays, for example.

"J.D., can you watch Justin for a little bit?" my grandmother told me before she left. "Granddad will be in the living room doing some paperwork."

"Why can't Vanessa do it?" I asked.

"She's going with your mother to the beauty supply store, since you used up your mother's perm," Grandma said. "They'll be back in a bit."

Ugh. They knew I had tons of homework I needed to finish before school on Monday. How was I going to do it if I had to waste time watching Justin?

I told Justin to come with me to my bedroom.

As I looked over at him playing with his race

cars on the floor, I thought back to what Jordan had told me during our last game of Madden.

Maybe I should just take my mom's clippers and shave my head bald.

But I had never cut hair before.

I looked down at Justin. He had plenty of hair.

"Justin," I said. "Do you like your long hair?"

Justin pulled at the tip of one of his braids and paused. He scrunched his nose.

"No!" he yelled. I took that as a sign.

"Let's go into the bathroom for a little bit," I said. "I want to teach you a new game. It's called Barbershop."

Justin looked up at me and smiled like I had just invited him to the Meridian Bowling Alley. Mom was an expert bowler and it was her favorite way to blow off steam.

She even had her own ball with her initials engraved on it.

"If I bowl three hundred one more time, I'm going pro!" she'd yell after each strike.

The bowling alley had rides and games for kids, too. Justin loved going.

I sat my little brother down in the bathroom, put

a bedsheet around his neck, and spun him around in front of the mirror.

I grabbed my mom's clippers and turned them on. They buzzed.

There were eight different sizes of guard in the box, and I used the same size guard my mom used on me, a size two. I knew the larger numbers were

for straighter hair. If no hair came off, then you used a smaller number. I steadied Justin's head and I cut his hair into a fade.

Tradition be gone! Cornrows no more!

It didn't look half-bad. Plus, Justin was only three, so what did he care?

"Hey!" he said when he checked out his hair in the mirror. "Looks like Spider-Man's!" he yelled out as he walked around the bathroom pretending like he was shooting webs out of his hands.

I couldn't believe I did it.

And Justin looked so happy with how it all turned out.

Making Justin happy with something *I* did filled me with a warm feeling. Like I'd just finished a plate of fried fish and French fries that my mom made every Saturday in the summer.

This was proof that I could fix my own hair.

"Now watch this, Justin," I told him. "I'm going to cut mine."

I knew I could do it. Art was my thing. One time, I drew Black Panther, and my grandmother displayed it in the living room for everyone to see.

Hair was the same.

An art.

I took the clippers, looked in the mirror, and thought about how everyone would react once they saw my sick fade.

I turned them on with the size two guard, the same size I used on Justin.

I was going in the direction of my hair, starting at the crown of my head.

"You are great," I told myself. "You are dope. You are cutting your own hair."

I was the man.

I looked in the mirror as my mountaintops became a flat field. I finally DID look like Michael B. Jordan!

My heart pounded as I waited in my bedroom with Justin for my mom to get home.

As soon as I heard the door open and Mom and Vanessa come inside, I put baseball caps on both my and my brother's heads. I was afraid she'd be SO angry at me.

Justin burst out of my bedroom.

"Mom!" he said as he hugged her. My Bulldogs

cap almost covered his whole tiny head.

"Where's J.D.?" she said. At least that's what I heard as I hid out in my room.

I had cut Justin's hair without permission. Would I be grounded? Would this mean no more staying over at Jordan's house? Would Granddad make me read him more dry books? Or worse, would my mom tell me no peewee football this year?

I came out from my room slowly and sat down next to Justin on the couch in front of our only working TV.

Granddad had finished his paperwork and was watching reruns of *Jeopardy!*

"What is *The Color Purple*?" He yelled out the answer about a category named "The Oscars."

"J.D., now you got Justin wearing a hat, too!" he bellowed. "Boys, take those off!"

I did as I was told. When Justin didn't respond, I pulled off his hat.

Mom and Vanessa joined us next to Granddad on the couch. My mom's mouth dropped open when she saw my and Justin's new haircuts.

"Wow," she said, in shock. No one made a sound

for a really long time. Then finally, she continued, "I wish you had asked me if you could cut Justin's hair first."

I knew it. I might as well start collecting books to read to Granddad.

Then, Mom's face got softer.

"But Justin's hair does look pretty good, J.D. Your hair looks good, too," she said.

She looked at Justin and rubbed his cheek.

"Do you like your hair, baby?" she asked.

Justin burrowed into my mom's side and giggled.

"I think that's a yes," she said. "If you're this good at cutting your own hair, then that's one less thing I need to do every week."

I couldn't believe it!

"Your hair looks way better than before," Vanessa added. "Now you might not get put on punishment for using Mom's perm box."

My shoulders relaxed and I turned my attention back to *Jeopardy!*

That night, I went to sleep eagerly awaiting the school day on Monday. Now NO ONE would have anything bad to say about my hair.

CHAPTER 7
The Grand Reveal

Jordan seemed extra amped when he saw me show up in my ball cap again at the bus stop. I wanted my new hairline to be a surprise to everyone.

"What you got going on under there today, J.D.?" he asked. "Fake dreads? Did you dye them yellow like Lil Wayne?"

He knocked my cap off like I knew he would.

But when he saw my head, he said nothing.

Ah, the sweet sound of silence.

"Wow, your hair looks really good today," Jordan finally said. "Who did it? Did your mom take you to Henry Jr.'s?"

"No," I told him. "I did it myself."

Jordan smirked.

I rode the school bus in peace.

I changed classes in peace.

"I like your hair today," Jessyka told me at lunch.

Even better, when I got my Reading test back from Ms. Scott, not only did I get an A, but she said, "Did you get a haircut recently, J.D.? It looks nice!"

I was in heaven.

CHAPTER 8
My First Client

Day after day, my hair looked amazing. No one could crack on me anymore. The more I cut my own hair, the more I had fun with it. I tried all kinds of new things: fades, Caesars, baldies, I even cut parts into my head. And my hairline was always perfectly straight.

One Saturday, I was in my bedroom giving myself a new haircut when I heard a loud knock on the back door. My door led to the porch, and it had a screen that let me see outside without others being able to see in.

That meant I could always pretend I wasn't home if I didn't want to be bothered or let people in without anyone else knowing.

"Hey, J.D., let me in!"

It was Jordan.

I turned off my clippers, opened the back door,

and we snuck into my nearly empty bedroom.

"What else do you need besides a bed and a mirror?" Mom always responded when I tried to ask for new things.

Seeing Jordan here was strange. He never wanted to hang at my house. He always said there was nothing to do and it was too hot.

"What's up, Jordan?" I asked.

Jordan took off his red-and-black Chicago Bulls snapback.

His hair was a jagged pile of mess. He looked like someone had put a bowl on his head before doing a lineup, and then a tiger came along and smacked the bowl off with its claws.

My first instinct was to make fun of him, like he had done to me.

BUT.

My mom and grandparents made sure I had what they called "home training," and I just couldn't make fun of Jordan. Instead, I sensed an opportunity.

"Wow, Jordan, what happened to your hair?" I asked.

"My brother's out of town, and I tried to do it

myself, like you," he said. "I can't go outside like this!"

Jordan paced around the room like he expected that tiger to come back and finish the job.

"You've got to fix it, J.D."

I inspected his head. Jordan really had no idea what he was doing. His brother Naija might have had skills, but Jordan clearly didn't.

"Why don't you just go to Henry's?" I asked, already knowing the answer.

"Because I wouldn't leave until nighttime!" he shrieked. "I need to fix this before the football game comes on TV at four."

"Sit down in the chair," I told him. "Your hair is jacked, but I can fix it."

I picked up my clippers and went to work.

Hmm, it was one thing to cut my hair or Justin's hair. Even though Jordan was my friend, I felt kinda nervous. I knew I had to concentrate extra hard not to make any mistakes.

"J.D.," Jordan said, "you are always good with things in your hands. Pencils, footballs, game controllers, now clippers!"

"Yeah, well, not everybody has every toy

like you, Jordan, so sometimes pencils are good enough."

"You know what's not good enough?" Jordan asked.

I kept cutting his hair, listening.

"I just can't stand going outside if I don't have on new clothes or if I'm not chopped up," Jordan said. "I gotta look good all the time."

I liked Jordan's style, but sometimes it felt like he took it too seriously.

"If you got your clothes out of a box, you'd forget about that stuff," I said. "Clothes just get dirty anyway."

Jordan sighed. "Want to know the truth?" he asked.

I nodded because I was curious.

"At least you know people like you for you, not your things!" he said. "Sometimes I wonder if anyone would care about me if I didn't have the newest video games."

Jordan and I were quiet as I kept working. Sometimes being a good friend was about talking, but other times it was about listening.

By the time I was finished, Jordan had a perfect baldie with the logo of the Chicago Bulls on one side and a Jumpman on the other, just like I'd drawn in my notebook hundreds of times before.

It was a masterpiece.

"Wait," I said, "one more thing."

I pulled out a set of art pencils my grandmother had brought home from the rec center. I traced Jordan's designs with one black pencil and one red.

Jordan couldn't help but give me my props.

"Yo, J.D., this is dope," he said. "You're even better than my brother. I owe you!"

I hadn't thought about this part. If Henry Jr. and Naija got paid, why shouldn't I? Especially when my work was dope.

"Well, why don't you slide me three dollars for the job? Less than half of what they charge at Henry's," I said.

Jordan placed three crisp bills into my hands.

I couldn't believe I got Jordan to give me money!

I thought about all the things you can do with three dollars in Meridian, Mississippi. Even though Meridian was a town of ones—one mall, one barbershop, one high school, one middle school, and one elementary school—three dollars could get you far. You could:

Buy thirty pieces of ten-cent candy from the candy store!

30 x $0.10 = $3.00

Go to Miss Sweetie's House and buy her candy when the corner store was closed.

Go to the matinee and see a movie!

Three dollars was a lot of money, and I was RICH!!!

CHAPTER 9
The Start of a Business

Jordan's Chicago Bulls design got a lot of attention at school on Monday.

"Oh man! Did your brother do that?" Xavier asked.

"Nope, J.D. did," he said, throwing me a solid. "I only paid three dollars. He's open on Saturdays."

Hmm. More money. Two clients times three dollars each was six dollars. The newest Spider-Man comic cost $4.99. I just had to keep up with Jordan, Xavier, and Jessyka. Me and Jordan were super into the graphics, but Xavier and Jessyka had ALL the storylines memorized.

Six dollars would even leave me with one extra dollar for candy.

One dollar divided by ten cents was ten. I could buy ten pieces of candy with my extra dollar.

When Eddie, the quarterback on my peewee

football team, saw Jordan's designs at lunch, he said he wanted his hair cut by me, too. He always went to Hart and Son.

"I'm tired of waiting all day when I go!" he complained.

It didn't take long before I had a lot of clients. All the kids I played sports with and all the regular neighborhood kids wanted that fire I had with my clippers.

That very weekend, I set up my shop. It was really warm one day (like most days in Mississippi), so I put out a folding chair on the back porch. The rest of the time, I cut hair in my bedroom. I didn't have the kind of equipment you'd find at Henry's, so I improvised: I put a piece of toilet paper around my clients' necks and an old bedsheet over their clothes to keep the hair off. The sheet kept slipping, so I attached a hanger clip on the back to keep it in place.

Justin was my assistant barber. He swept up hair, collected money, and sometimes served as my hair model.

My mom and sister barely seemed to notice my

growing empire. The only complaint I heard was from my grandparents, who told all of us to stop using so much toilet paper. They knew I was cutting hair at home, but they didn't want me to cost THEM money while I was doing it.

"Do you think toilet paper is free?" my grandmother said.

I couldn't worry about toilet paper. My mind was busy counting money.

If I did ten haircuts a day, that equaled thirty dollars.

10 haircuts x $3.00 = $30.00

I imagined what I'd buy with all that cash: my own video game console, a television set, and all the candy I could eat.

Soon I would have every Marvel comic, except the Captain America ones. I didn't like those.

My bedroom would be the most tricked-out kids' barbershop ever!

Peewee football practice was always during the week, so I had all day Saturday to cut hair. One day, after I'd closed up shop, me and Xavier, Jordan, and

Eddie were in my room talking about everything from the newest videos on House of Highlights to what plays Coach Sidney had tried to teach us for next week.

"Yes, next week I'm going to stop pitching it to the running back so much. Coach said I can practice some quarterback sneaks," Eddie said.

"Why don't you throw the ball to me more?" Xavier asked.

"Because Jessyka is a better wide receiver!" Eddie laughed.

Mom was out with Vanessa at her track meet, Grandma was at the studio center teaching a kids' ceramics class. The only one home was Granddad, who was practicing piano before he headed out to sell burial insurance. He'd leave as soon as Grandma and Mom got back home.

I could hear Vanessa and Mom burst through the door and then I heard an extra voice. It was Jessyka. She must've come home with Vanessa today.

"I have to help Mom bring in the laundry," I heard Vanessa say. "Just wait for me inside a few minutes," she told Jessyka.

I heard footsteps down the hall and saw a shadow approaching my doorframe. That's when Jessyka appeared in her warmup suit.

"What are you all doing in here?" she asked.

"This is my barbershop," I said. "It's where I've been cutting all the guys' hair."

"Yeah, Jessyka, NO GIRLS ALLOWED!" Xavier said.

I turned to Xavier and gave him a look.

"No, Xavier, Jessyka can be here," I said. "It's my room anyway."

Jessyka jogged in and looked at my barber station.

"Can I sit in your chair?" Jessyka asked.

"Sure." I turned to Eddie and said, "Get up, Eddie."

Eddie looked annoyed.

"You're not done with my edge up, J.D., and I never saw a girl at Henry Jr.'s place. Maybe I should go back there," Eddie said.

I had to let Eddie know that this was MY shop.

"Well, this isn't Hart and Son!" I said. "I make the rules."

Eddie got up and Jessyka sat down.

"Sometimes I wish I could cut bangs, but my mom won't let me," she said, pulling at a strand of her hair and fake cutting it with her fingers.

"I bet I could do it," I said. "But your mom might get mad, so why don't you ask her first and come back next week?"

Jessyka grinned the way she did when she caught the ball on a crossing route, broke a couple of tackles, and was off to the end zone. The sideline, the coaches, and the crowd always screamed EXTRA loud when she scored.

"That's not a bad idea," she said.

Jessyka stood up and got out of the chair and looked at all of us.

"I've got to go, but I'll see you all on the field."

We heard Jessyka walk down the hall. When she reached the end of it, she yelled back, "I'm so fast, they won't be able to catch me!"

Jordan, Eddie, and Xavier all groaned, but I laughed. Jessyka could teach all of us about throwing shade.

CHAPTER 10

Henry Hart Jr. Has a Problem

I loved everything about peewee football. There were lots of kids on it who went to both Douglass and Catholic school.

Since I was cutting the hair of most of the guys on my team, Meridian's Mighty Mice looked extra clean. We came up with a plan for everyone to take off their helmets after a touchdown and show off their haircuts. Jessyka even got my sister to style her hair different. It was obvious that all the guys were getting their hair cut somewhere that was not Henry's. He never took special requests. No parts, no color, no hi-tops and no dreadlocks. I don't think he hated these styles, he just didn't know how to do them, especially not on a kid.

"Check this out, Dad," my friend Xavier said after he scored a touchdown. He took off his helmet in the end zone. I had cut a picture of Mighty Mouse into the back of Xavier's head, which was always in his normal hi-top fade. I had even colored it with my art pencils.

I usually recognized most of the people who came to my games. But this time I had the weird feeling of being watched. Whenever we scored a touchdown or made an exciting play on offense, all the parents and friends in the bleachers would stand up and cheer. I played linebacker, so I was not on the field when we scored and could see one person in the bleachers who kept his arms crossed and stayed seated. He was wearing a knit cap and sunglasses–it was Henry Jr. I was sure of it. What was he up to?

His kids were little, so he had no reason to be there. What else could he have been doing except trying to find out where all his kid clients were getting their hair cut?

"J.D.!" Eddie yelled to me after the game was over. "That dude Henry Jr. from the barbershop was asking me who cut my hair . . . I told him it was you."

»»««

GO TEAM

After the game, I waited for my family to find me to avoid Henry Jr. in the bleachers. My grandparents, Justin, and Vanessa were the only ones who came to my games, but Mom had taken a night off from studying for her exams to watch me in action.

"Another win, Mom!" I said. My whole family caught up with me on the sidelines.

"Yes, and I can see you've been cutting a lot of hair while I've been out of the house," Mom said as she squatted down and hugged me.

"Yeah, J.D., not bad. But I bet you can't do girls' hair," Vanessa said. "Did you see how good Jessyka looked out there?"

She always had something to say!

We piled into our car and as it rolled down the street, I could only think about Henry Jr. and what he wanted.

CHAPTER 11
The Visit

Everyone in Meridian knows everything about everyone else. And even if they don't know, it's easy enough to ask a friend, a neighbor, or a fellow churchgoer the right question to get any answer.

So it wasn't that big of a surprise when one Saturday night, long after I'd closed up my bedroom barbershop, I found Henry Jr. knocking on the back porch. Of course he figured out how to find me.

Even though it was getting dark outside, he still had the same knit cap and dark sunglasses he had worn at my football game.

"Hello, Jay Jay," he said.

No one except my family called me James. Definitely not "Jay Jay." He was trying to get me mad, and it was working.

"I know what you're up to with your little underground barbershop," Henry Jr. said.

This was unbelievable! Why was Henry Jr. at my house worried about what I was doing?

"Hi, Mr. Henry Jr.," I said to him. "What can I help you with? Should I get my mom?"

It seemed like Henry Jr. was sweating. I couldn't really tell. He always seemed kinda out of breath, but today it was worse. It was almost as if I could see smoke coming out of his ears!

"Don't worry about your mom right now, but if you don't knock it off," he said in a louder voice, "I'm going to call the authorities and get you shut down!"

Could he do that? How?

"You don't have any type of license to do anything!" he said, as if he could read my mind. "Your mom worked at the hospital; she knows about the Department of Health!"

Before I could even respond, he stormed off.

He had to be kidding. Who would believe an eight-year-old kid had his own barbershop? And how could it be illegal anyway? Half the kids I knew got their hair cut at home.

Henry Jr. was just a big hater. I didn't have time for haters—I had a business to run, money to make, and clients who depended on me!

CHAPTER 12

Henry Jr. Makes Good on His Threat

I went about the rest of my week as usual–school, football practice, and church. There was no sign of Henry Jr. anywhere. No one lurking in the bushes, no strange people at the football field or standing outside my house.

On Saturday morning, I was prepping for Xavier as Justin played with his Lightning McQueen toy from the movie *Cars*.

Xavier stood right beside my workstation. This week, he wanted an edge up with a small 'fro like Steph Curry, and I was ready to try it.

"I grew my hair out for two weeks just like you said," he told me as he sat in my chair.

I grabbed my clippers.

"Man, I wish I had caught the winning touchdown last week instead of Jessyka," Xavier said.

"It's not fair, why is Jessyka on our team anyway? She's the only girl!"

Xavier loves to win, and I could tell this had been bothering him.

"She's good, Xavier. She's been in sports from the time she could walk, I think. Plus her dad played football in college and they practice catching the ball and running routes ALL THE TIME!"

Xavier sat quietly, looking at the mirror like he was thinking.

I knew what it felt like to want to be the best at something. And I bet Jessyka knew, too. They should just talk.

Before I could suggest it or even finish Xavier's cut, I heard someone pounding at the door. It sounded like Jordan. He's big enough to knock that loudly. Plus, he always likes to be first.

Boom! Boom! Boom!

I peered out the door. The person outside was not Jordan. It was a man in a button-down short-sleeved shirt, church pants, and church shoes. He was carrying a clipboard.

"Is this the house of Mr. and Mrs. Slayton Evans?"

"Who wants to know?" I asked.

"Well, I need to speak to an adult, young man," he said. He handed me a business card that read:

ROBERT VICTOR

County Health Inspector

Meridian Lauderdale County Health Department

5224 Valley Street, Meridian, MS 39307

Phone: 601-123-4567

"I was told an unlicensed barbershop was operating out of this home," he continued.

"*Well*, my *grandparents* aren't here," I said. It was true. Granddad was visiting burial insurance clients and Saturday was a busy day for Grandma's ceramics classes. That's when most people could go. Mom had gone shopping with Vanessa. My family trusted me enough to leave me alone for an hour or two.

Mr. Victor pushed past me, and I tried to block him. It didn't work. He just barged right in!

I was busted.

"I'm going to need all you little fellas to get

home to your parents right now," Mr. Victor said to Xavier and Justin.

I guess he thought Justin was another one of my clients.

"Can you wait for J.D. to finish my edge up? I'll look terrible if I walk out like this," Xavier said.

Mr. Victor let out a smug little laugh. His belly jiggled over his belt buckle.

"No, son," he replied. "You have to leave now. I suggest you get your hairline finished at the real

barbershop in town, Hart and Son. They have a license."

That stung. I might not have a license, but my skills were way better than Henry Jr.'s.

Mr. Victor explained that this was a warning. If he came by again and my business was open, he'd talk to my grandparents and I'd be in real trouble.

When he was done with his lecture, he spun around on his shiny black shoes and marched out the door.

Henry Jr. had gone through with his threat. I had to figure out how to get him back and stop him from destroying my life.

CHAPTER 13

The Little Barber Strikes Back

After my mom got home with Vanessa, my entire family sat down in the kitchen for dinner like we always did on weekends. This time there was steak, rice, and collard greens that had been simmering all morning

Normally, I would have been on my second helping, but I just couldn't stop thinking about Mr. Victor and his threat. I used my fork to push the food around my plate.

"Eat your greens, J.D.," my mom said.

"I want another piece of cornbread first," I told her.

"J.D., is something wrong?" she asked. "It's not like you to talk back, and never have you ever been this silent around my food."

How did she always know when something was bothering me? I shoveled the rest of my greens into my mouth, pretending they tasted like the candy I had bought with all my barbershop money. I didn't want her to ask any more questions.

"J.D. has a new video game console in his bedroom," Vanessa said.

My mom looked at me, shocked.

I had been able to keep my full-blown barbershop a secret from her because she had lots of exams to finish up her MBA. Kids' track was in the morning on Saturdays, so Vanessa hadn't entirely caught on to what I was doing, either.

"Well, Mom, people have been paying me for their haircuts and I saved enough money to buy it myself," I told her.

"That explains all the kids that have been running in and out of this house all weekend," Granddad said. "Your grandmother and I were just talking about that with your mother."

They all turned to look at one another. Granddad shook his head and smiled.

"Wow, I guess I have a little Henry Jr. on my hands!" Mom said. "I will tell your uncle Hal to put a pair of clippers in the box next time he sends clothes."

I cringed inside when Mom mentioned Henry Jr.'s name. I also wasn't too excited about getting a new set of hand-me-downs, but an extra set of clippers sounded cool.

I was happy Mom wasn't mad at my business. I didn't need another person trying to shut me down. If it was up to Henry Jr., I'd be out of business before I barely got a start!

After dinner, I couldn't sleep. And for once, it wasn't all the candy I ate.

I hardly had any left in my candy jar, which was looking almost empty. How would I ever be able to afford more? Or the newest video games? And comic books? I would be back at Jordan's house using all his toys and gadgets just like before. Mom always told me that we had everything we needed and it wasn't polite to expect others to just give us stuff. But with my barbershop, I could work for all those extras I wanted. Plus it made me feel special. No one else at school could do what I did!

Why would a grown man care so much about one kid cutting hair in his bedroom?

B
BATTLE
??

And what could I do to stop him?

I cut kids' hair better and cheaper than him and that's why he was mad.

That was his fault!

I had to figure out a way to keep Henry Jr. from trying to destroy me.

Maybe I could sneak into his barbershop and put superglue in between his scissors.

Maybe I could replace all his cleaning solution with the blue Gatorade we used at peewee football.

Who was I kidding? All my ideas were terrible. I needed to team up with someone to think of something great. I knew just the person!

CHAPTER 14

The Plan

"What could he want from a kid?" I asked Jordan. I told him about Henry Jr. snooping on me.

We sat in a tent in his backyard. It was the best place for thinking. I grabbed a flashlight and each time it lit up, you could see the football paint I put under my eyes.

"Man, whatever," he said. "Forget that dude."

"I can't forget him! He's trying to shut down my barbershop! We have to come up with a plan to stop him. Do you want dope haircuts or not?"

After years of playing Madden with Jordan, I knew he had good ideas in his head. I beat him *most* of the time, but not *always*.

"What if we send him a letter and tell him it's from the health department and *he's* about to be shut down?"

"Ain't gonna work," Jordan said. "He knows the rules."

"What if I sneak into his store and put dishwashing liquid in his shampoo and bubbles in his shaving cream can?" I tried next.

"Nope, ain't gonna work," Jordan said. "You just going to end up in juvie."

"Well, are you going to think of something or just say 'Ain't gonna work' to everything I say?!" I shouted.

"Maybe if you think of something that WILL work, then I'll say something different," he replied.

We both paused and stared at the flashlight. "Why don't you just challenge him to some kind of game like we do in football every week?"

I smiled. Jordan had come up with the beginning of a good idea.

"Yeah, like a barber competition," I said excitedly.

"We'll invite the whole town," Jordan added. "If you win, you get to keep cutting hair in your bedroom and he has to leave you alone."

"Now *that* sounds like a plan," I said.

I turned off the flashlight. On the walk home, I let the plan fully develop in my mind.

CHAPTER 15
The Challenge

The next day at school, during computer class, I secretly typed up a note for Henry Jr., printed it, and grabbed the paper from the printer before the teacher could notice.

I thought if Henry Jr. received a typed-up message, it would make me look serious, like I really meant business.

One afternoon, right before I knew Hart and Son was about to close, I walked down to the shop and slid the note under the door.

Henry Jr.:

If you want me to stop cutting hair in my room, then you need to beat me in a competition.

If I win, you will leave me alone.

If you win, I will stop cutting hair.

P.S. I make the rules. You agree to them.

CHECK ☐ YES OR ☐ NO

YOU KNOW WHERE TO FIND ME.

»»««

The next week after our peewee football game, Eddie passed *me* a piece of paper.

“Henry Jr. gave this to my dad. He said it’s for you,” Eddie said. “I don’t know what it’s about, but here.”

Eddie, the only kid our age bigger than Jordan, had stopped going to Hart and Son, but his dad still went every week. Henry Jr. was trying to find a connection to me. I read the paper in my hands.

Henry Jr. had checked the “Yes” box.

CHAPTER 16
The Rules

To be honest, I didn't expect Henry Jr. to agree to my terms without hearing more details. But he did, and now I had to come up with the rules of the barber competition.

The first rule was easy: Make sure nothing took place during a football game of any kind—peewee, college, or NFL. I wanted the whole town to be there.

"Good idea, J.D., you'll blow up for sure after you beat him in front of everyone."

"Right," I said. "More customers, more money."

"So who are you going to get to judge this?" Jordan asked.

I hadn't thought about that yet.

"I don't know," I said. "The crowd?"

"That ain't gonna work," Jordan replied. That must be his favorite thing to say!

"What if he invites more people than you?"

I hadn't thought of that, either.

"You're right," I said. "I'll have to think about it some more."

The next time my whole family ate dinner together, I decided I had to tell them about the upcoming competition. If I wanted everyone to come, I had to give them enough notice.

"I have something to tell you."

Everyone stopped mid-bite and looked up at me.

"In two weeks, I'm having a barber competition at Hart and Son. Since I started cutting hair in my bedroom I've been getting real good at it. Now I want the whole town to know I'm the best barber in the city."

Granddad shuffled in his seat. Grandma's eyes darted around the table as if she could not believe what she was hearing.

Vanessa tried to stifle her laughter.

"I'm serious, Vanessa, I cut hair and I make money."

Vanessa took a long, slow drink of water.

"How are you really going to beat a grown man

at cutting hair?" she asked. "And why would he want to challenge YOU anyway?"

"It's a long story," I said. I didn't really want to tell them about the health inspector and get in trouble. "It will be amazing, though. The whole town will be there. The only thing I need is a judge."

That's when Grandma piped in.

"Well, one of my ceramics students, Mrs. Holiday, owns the beauty school in town. Maybe she and her husband can do it."

"Really, Grandma?" I said excitedly. "That would be so cool!"

"I'm sure she'd be happy to do it." Grandma dabbed her mouth with a napkin and continued. She said she's been giving art classes in Meridian for so long that by now everyone owed her a favor.

I told them the rest of the rules I had thought of: I wanted to pull hairstyles out of a hat and have a best of three rounds with thirty minutes for each style. Mom said she was really impressed by my plan. Vanessa cleared her throat loudly, and Justin clapped. Granddad was busy eating, but I could tell he was proud, too.

This was just the boost I needed!

I delivered the rules to Henry Jr. first thing on a Saturday morning before the last regular college football game of the season.

He read the rules silently.

"All right, little man. Just let me know the time and day and I'll be ready," he said. "I'm going to teach you a lesson about trying to act grown."

I had no idea what he meant. But if anyone was going to be teaching lessons, it was me.

CHAPTER 17
Spreading the Hype

My grandmother took me to see Mr. and Mrs. Holiday at The Meridian School of Beauty after school to ask them to judge my contest.

"J.D. is going to be one of your ace students one day!" Grandma filled in Mr. and Mrs. Holiday on what we had talked about at dinner.

"Yes, Mrs. Holiday," I added, "I'm having a barber battle. Best two out of three wins."

"Well, that's quite a mind you have there," Mrs. Holiday said. "I like it!"

I had my judges! And they already liked me and my grandma!

"We'd have no problem judging the contest for you, young man, but we're going to be fair. Don't think just because I know your grandmother that I'm going to let you win!"

I looked around the room suspiciously. Could they hear my thoughts?

"I know I can win fair and square, Mrs. Holiday," I said. "Just make sure you invite the whole beauty school!"

Another suggestion Mr. and Mrs. Holiday had was that they should select the haircuts that me and Henry Jr. would pull out of a hat. That way, no one would be able to practice the day before. I wasn't worried.

With that figured out, I turned my focus to making sure we had an audience. My own head had worked to get kids to come to my house for haircuts. Now this barber competition would make me the most popular barber in all of Meridian!

I put signs all over my elementary school. I just copied something I'd seen on one of my boxing video games.

MERIDIAN'S FIRST
BARBER COMPETITION!

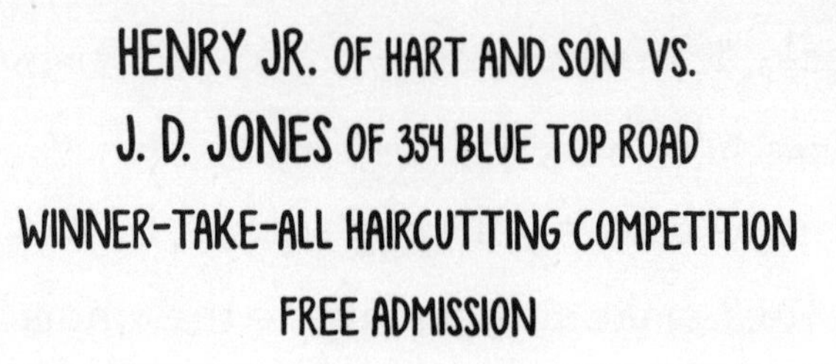

COME SEE WHO IS THE BEST BARBER IN THE CITY!

I put signs up on the church bulletin board and made sure it was in the church weekly announcements. The church paid my mom to type up the announcements, so on Saturday night, I asked her to include exactly what I wanted. I asked my granddad to give fliers to all his funeral insurance customers and Grandma to put signs all over her ceramics studio. I even gave my sister fliers for her friends! My mom took fliers to her school. And just to be safe, I got on my bike and delivered fliers to the peewee football squad and my coach.

Once I beat Henry Jr., I'd have every client in the whole city!

CHAPTER 18
The Night Before

When this kind of thing happens in movies or books, you see that on the night before the competition, the competitors can't sleep.

Well, not in this story.

I slept like a baby. I knew I had Henry Jr. right where I wanted him. I had done dozens of cuts. I knew what was in style. I knew I was fast—and good. And I knew that by the end of the day, all of Henry Jr.'s remaining clients would be mine.

In the morning, things were different. Even with a good night's sleep and the confidence of almost-certain victory, I was in a mood.

Unlike with my football games, my entire family would be at the battle. My mom even gave everyone a ride to Hart and Son. When we got there, I found out that I had forgotten my backup clippers from Uncle Hal. Mom had to drive me the ten minutes back to our house to get them. What a messy start.

On the way back to Hart and Son, I double-checked the supplies in my backpack. I had my clippers, backup clippers, a brush, and my set of art pencils.

I suddenly started to worry. In fact, I started to sweat. Henry Jr. probably had better clippers than I did. He had a whole barbershop of tools! I didn't remember to put what type of equipment we could use in my rules.

My clippers were from JCPenney. My granddad had gotten them with his discount from when he was the head manager there. Henry Jr. got his stuff from special salespeople who came to his shop. I could only go to Sally Beauty Supply if I wanted something extra!

I wished I had spent less of the money I earned on making the barbershop fun and cool.

My mom looked at me as I nervously clutched my backpack.

"Are you okay, J.D.?" she asked.

"Well, Mom, I'm a little scared," I said.

"Do you still want to do this?" she asked.

"I have to, Mom, the whole CITY is coming!"

"Well, YOU were built for this moment. You're my child, J.D. We Joneses don't let nerves stop us!"

She was right. Mom went back to school even though she was nervous. Choir made me nervous at first and now it's just normal. I had even stopped lip-synching.

"But I'll tell you a secret," Mom said. "Back when I ran track, I sometimes used to feel like throwing up before a big race! But then I'd envision myself crossing the finish line first and everyone cheering, and that helped me keep calm."

That's how I felt now. Like throwing up!

"Even worse," Mom continued, "when I was training to be a nurse, the first time I had to draw blood from someone's arm, I was so afraid that I would hit the wrong vein and the patient would die! Is there any chance someone's going to die while you cut their hair today?"

"No, Mom, there isn't," I said, laughing. I could tell she was joking.

Mom could be really funny sometimes.

"Then don't be nervous. Just look out at the crowd and imagine everyone clapping for YOU!"

The plan was for me and Henry Jr. to select our own hair models. We'd each gotten three different kids to grow their hair out to the same length.

But when I arrived, Mrs. Holiday threw us a curveball.

"Hello Henry Jr. and J.D.!" she greeted us outside the shop.

"I had the best idea last night! Wouldn't it be

more fun and exciting if *I* picked one of the models?!" She seemed so pleased with her idea, but I didn't like it one bit.

"That way it will be fairer," she continued. "Every now and then my beauty school students practice on local kids, and I called two of them in."

Then she directed her attention to me.

"If you want to be a great barber one day, J.D., you're going to have to know how to cut ALL types of hair!"

All types of hair? The only hair I had cut that was not like mine was my friend Xavier's. What did Mrs. Holiday have in mind? Was I supposed to know how to cut girl hair, too? Or straight hair? I had planned on using Xavier, Eddie, and Jordan as my models. I already knew how to cut their hair.

I couldn't tell what Henry Jr. thought of the new rule. His face looked kind of blank. He probably wasn't worried because, at the end of the day, he had years of experience.

Was there a chance I could lose in front of all my family and friends?

CHAPTER 19
The Barber Competition

As worried as I felt on the inside, on the outside, I looked as clean as a star at his movie premiere. At least as clean as I could with my best church shirt and shoes. I brought a jar of candy for the audience and made sure that Jordan, with all of his gadgets, was able to play music and set up a microphone for Mr. and Mrs. Holiday.

Hart and Son only had two barber chairs and one small bench for the people who were waiting. I got permission from my gym teacher to bring a bunch of folding chairs, but there still weren't enough seats for everyone.

The only time I had performed in front of a crowd by myself was during the school Christmas play in second grade when I played Joseph. I dropped the fake baby Jesus when I was handing the doll to the girl who played Mary and everyone laughed. Being on stage in front of people was nothing like being on the football team when no one could even tell who you were!

People gathered outside the barbershop with some pressing their noses against the glass. Jordan quickly hooked up his sound system so folks could hear the announcements outside.

It felt like a tailgate party at Tuskegee University.

My entire family sat in the front row like a line of ducks dressed in their Sunday finest. They were next to Henry Sr. and Henry Jr.'s wife and two little kids. I noticed all of my friends, especially Jessyka sitting by her mom. She waved, flashing her bright blue fingernails, and walked up to me.

"You'll crush it, J.D. Just like I did in football last game." Before she went back to her seat, she added, "And when my mom sees you cut hair, I know she'll let you cut my bangs."

That's just what I needed to hear!

I saw Justin fussing on my mom's lap and decided to go calm him. Vanessa was there, too, and she had this weird look in her eyes. I couldn't tell if she was happy for me, jealous, or nervous. But then she grabbed my arm.

"You got this, J.D.," she said.

Next to her, Grandma and Granddad matched for the occasion, with Grandma in a powder-blue church hat and Granddad in a powder-blue tie. They both smiled at me.

Everyone I cared about had come out to cheer me on.

A photographer from the *Meridian City Times* took a photo of me and Henry Jr. for the newspaper. The flash was so bright, I felt dizzy!

Just then, Mrs. Holiday's voice crackled over the speaker.

"Welcome, everyone, to Meridian's first barber battle!" Mrs. Holiday announced. Me and Henry Jr. got into our stations.

"Give it up for our brave and talented contestants, Mr. Henry Hart Jr. and Little Mr. J. D. Jones!"

Mrs. Holiday paused for applause. I tried to imagine that all the cheers were for me, just like Mom said.

"Now, the competition is best two out of three.

My husband and I will serve as the professional judges, but everyone is allowed to participate by using the numbers underneath your seats. You can rate the haircuts from one to five, five being the best and one being, well, not so good."

She rolled up her sleeves. Mrs. Holiday reminded me of the gymnast Simone Biles in the nylon track-suit she always wore to keep from getting dirty with hair supplies.

"Now give it up for our hair models! Let's hope they all go home happy!"

Xavier, Eddie, and this kid from church named Steve walked out. Steve's parents were strict, even stricter than my family, so he was not in football or any extracurricular activities. How was I going to cut all his hair?!

I did not know Henry Jr.'s models very well either. Maybe they were his relatives from another town over? Two of them had small Afros and Mrs. Holiday's "wild card" model was another kid with a long, bushy Afro. Mrs. Holiday mentioned that her models grew out their hair for the battle!

"Okay, let's begin," Mrs. Holiday said.

Our styling tool of choice was a set of clippers with a guard—no shears. We'd have thirty minutes to complete each style before clippers down.

"My husband, Billy, or Mr. Holiday to all of you, will kick things off by pulling the first style out of the hat."

Mr. Holiday, a short and burly man, walked over to the hat and pulled out a piece of paper.

"The first style is . . . a fade!"

Our clippers buzzed on. I worked on Eddie's head and felt less nervous as I concentrated on the haircut. But I could sense that Henry Jr. was working faster than me. How many hundreds of basic fades had he cut over his lifetime?!

"Clippers down!" I heard Mrs. Holiday say.

Out the side of my eye, I saw her whispering to Mr. Holiday. Henry Jr. had finished before me and it looked pretty good. Mine was good, too, but the back edge was a little unfinished.

"We must give this round to Mr. Henry Jr.! What does the crowd think?"

When Mrs. Holiday asked the crowd to rate Henry Jr.'s fade, he got mostly fours and fives. I got

mostly fours. The only fives were from my family!

Mrs. Holiday pulled the next style out of the hat herself and addressed the crowd.

"Our next haircut is . . . a pompadour!"

I heard the crowd shift in their seats. Not everybody seemed to know what that was, but I did! Celebrities like Miguel, Bruno Mars, and Janelle Monáe had all tried their own versions of pompadours.

Luckily, Xavier was up next in my chair. All I needed to do was add the right styling product and then edge up his sides.

Henry Jr. was trying to straighten his model's hair, but he didn't finish in time to make the edges neat.

The Holidays whispered to each other again.

"We think the winner of this round is J.D.!"

This time the crowd gave me mostly fives and fours and Henry Jr. got threes, twos, and even a couple ones!

"For this competition's last style," Mrs. Holiday said, "could I please have Henry Sr., the longtime owner of this shop, come to the front to make the selection?"

Henry Sr. unfolded his long, sticklike legs and reached his wiry hand into the upside-down baseball cap.

"Hi-top fade!" he yelled out. "Dunno what in the world that is, but good luck, boys." Henry Sr. shuffled back to his chair.

I knew exactly what a hi-top fade was. I wasn't so sure that Henry Jr. did. Either way, we were both cutting the hair of a new client for the first time.

Henry Jr. calmly buzzed off the bushy ponytail of the kid in his chair. He was already ahead!

My clippers buzzed as I shaved off Steve's ponytail, but as soon as his hair hit the floor, my clippers stopped working! I heard a few gasps from the crowd, and my mom covered her mouth with her hand.

I walked over to my bag and whipped out my uncle's backup clippers. I'd never used them before, but if I wanted to win, I had to think back to what Mom said on our car ride—we Joneses never give up.

The good thing about Steve having so much hair was that I could really do something extra special with my hi-top fade, like a slightly uneven look with one side higher.

I stole a quick glance at Henry Jr. It looked like he was trying to copy me!

Back on Steve's head, I was feeling pretty good about what I was doing. I focused on the haircut the way I did when I got sucked into my drawings.

Even if I lost, I wanted to make sure I did a good job and everyone knew I could cut hair just as good as Henry Jr. That was important to me.

CHAPTER 20
The Winner?

"Clippers down!" Mrs. Holiday said into the microphone.

Thirty minutes after Henry Sr. announced the style we had to cut, the last competition was over. The clean R&B music Jordan had been playing for us through the sound system stopped. I put my clippers down and looked at my work. I had cut the word "Winner" into the back of Steve's head and traced the outline of the words with my gold art pencil. I felt so proud.

I started dusting the extra hair off Steve's shoulders and spun him around to face the crowd.

Henry Jr. spun his model around, too . . . but the crowd gasped, and not in a good way.

Instead of an even hi-top fade, Henry Jr. had somehow cut the top of his model's hair into a U shape. It looked like someone had bitten the top of the kid's head, as if it were a hamburger.

Mrs. Holiday walked over to her husband hesitantly. They started whispering again, and I could tell they were in shock.

"Well now," she said. "We think the clear winner is J.D. for this round."

Everyone in the crowd gave me fives. Even Henry Sr. held up a score of five, before his daughter-in-law smacked the card out of his hands.

"And the winner of the entire competition is Mr. James Jones, everybody!"

I had won. I was the Master Barber of Meridian! Henry Jr. had to leave me alone. He had to keep his promise.

I looked out at the crowd. My family was clapping loudly, and some people were even chanting "Go, J.D.!"

I felt amazing.

But then I saw how sad Henry Jr.'s family looked. His wife was on the verge of tears!

That didn't feel so great.

5
5
5
5

CHAPTER 21

A Real Job

After the competition, I got right back to my regularly scheduled programming of cutting hair in my bedroom.

Only this time, I had a line and had to take appointments, unlike before when it was first come, first served.

I started charging five dollars a pop. Shouldn't an award-winning barber make more than three bucks?

I was raking in the dough on Saturdays, cutting hair morning, noon, and night. The only problem was that I didn't even have time to spend it! Instead, Jordan, Eddie, Xavier, and a couple of other guys from the team enjoyed the riches. They'd eat candy and play video games while I cut twenty heads!

20 clients x $5.00 = $100.00

With so many kids in my room, it turned into an oven, so we moved the whole operation outside. I cut hair on my porch, and all the extra hair blew into our lawn.

"J.D.!" my grandmother yelled. "Don't you know all that hair in the grass attracts birds?!"

She was mad.

"Who is going to clean it up and who are all these kids coming in and out the house at all times of day?"

"I made a hundred dollars cash today, Grandma," I said.

The tone of Grandma's voice changed.

"Well, good boy, save your money. But try to figure out a way to cut hair without disrupting this house," she said. "And now you can pay me back for all the toilet paper you took."

In bed that night, I thought about my $100. If I could get out of church on Sundays, or at least get out of church EARLY on Sundays, I could get more. How many clients would I need to make $200 a weekend?

$200 ÷ $5 = 40 clients

The next day, Mom surprised us after church in the parking lot.

"Guess what, J.D.?" Mom beamed. "I got an A on my last management exam. That means I can graduate ahead of time!"

I gave my mom a BIG hug.

"Whoa, Mom! Does this mean you can apply for that job now?"

"Yes, I think so," she said.

The Joneses were doing great things.

To celebrate, Grandma and Granddad took us to the new buffet restaurant in town. I was so excited! I loved my mom's and grandma's cooking, but we NEVER, EVER ate out! This was something special.

Mom even said we could bring a friend, her treat.

"I want to bring Xavier!" I said.

"I'm taking Jessyka!" Vanessa added.

"Miles Morales!" Justin shouted. Mom didn't say the friend had to be real!

The New Meridian Buffet had only been open a few weeks. It still had a Grand Opening sign outside lined with colorful flags.

Whenever anything new came to Meridian, everyone went. Black, white, rich, poor–it was always an event.

My family each got their plates, and Xavier handed us kids ours. When he got to Jessyka, I heard him say something to her softly.

"Say, Jess, can I ask you a question?"

"Only my dad calls me Jess, Xavier, but you can ask me a question," Jessyka responded.

"Do you think I could practice running routes with you and your dad before school?" he asked.

Jessyka gave a side smile.

"We get up at six in the morning to play catch in my backyard. Are you sure you want to come over that early?"

Xavier seemed to nod with his whole body, not just his head. I was glad to see my friends on the same team for once.

We loaded our plates with delicious food and made our way to our table.

The New Meridian Buffet was crowded, so it wasn't that surprising to see Henry Jr. there. What was surprising was when he walked over to us.

Suddenly, my macaroni and cheese felt like a wet, floppy fish—the kind I caught when I went fishing with Xavier and his dad.

CHAPTER 22
Let's Make a Deal

"Oh, hi there, Mr. Henry," my mom said. "It's nice to see you again. We're just here celebrating that I'm almost done with school."

"More school, Ms. Jones? I see where your son gets his smarts." Henry Jr. nodded slightly at me and crouched by my seat.

"Hey, James," he said. "I have a proposal for you. Business is down, and I can't lose my shop. It's been a part of this town forever!"

I looked at Henry Jr. intently.

"I'm asking right here, in front of your whole family, to get your mom's and grandparents' permission. I know you have peewee football practice in the fall during the week and church on Sundays. Why don't you consider coming to work for me on Saturdays?"

He had tried to shut me down before with the

health inspector. He had tried to take away something that means so much to me.

Even so, I couldn't help feeling sorry for Henry Jr. Between my grandparents, church, weekly Bible study, and my mom, I knew I had to always TRY to be nice, even if someone had been unkind to me first.

"Well, we'll see Mr. Hart," I told him.

I decided I'd sleep on it. But first, I was going to enjoy the night with my family, celebrating my mom. I couldn't wait to watch her walk across the stage and graduate again.

Monday was my only night free from choir practice, peewee football, and Bible study, so that's when I went down to Hart and Son.

Henry didn't close shop until eight o'clock at night. I sat on his waiting bench, watching and watching and watching. No one came in after Henry Jr.'s last customer, so he decided to close early, at six o'clock. I guess business really was slow.

Henry Jr. looked into his tip jar to take inventory.

A tip jar. Why hadn't I thought of that?

"Thanks for coming, J.D.," Henry Jr. said.

He sat down in his barber chair looking like a squashed tomato.

"Now, look, I can't let my dad's legacy close on my watch," he said. "I want to propose something that lets us both win."

I had my own ideas of how we could both "win," but I let Henry Jr. go first.

"How much do you charge for cuts at your house, J.D.?" Henry Jr. asked.

"Three dollars before I won the competition. Five dollars after," I said.

Henry Jr. smirked. I think he was impressed by my business sense.

"Little J, you obviously have talent, and you know what kids want," he said. "I have to admit, I don't. And now everybody knows it.

"But what I do know is how to run a business. I can offer you a chair in my shop on weekends. Kids' haircuts are seven fifty a head and you can give me twenty-five dollars a week in chair rent. If you get good enough to cut adult hair you can charge more. You can even keep all the tips you make."

I looked around for a sheet of paper and a marker.

I was pretty good at math.

Home

20 heads per day x $5 = $100

$100 x 4 Saturdays = $400

Hart and Son

20 heads per day x $7.50 = $150

$150 x 4 Saturdays = $600

Monthly chair rent fee

$25 per week x 4 weeks per month = $100

$600–$100 =$500

I'd make an extra one-hundred dollars a month working at Hart and Son.

Plus I wouldn't have to worry about my grandmother complaining about kids coming in and out of the house, using her bedsheets as capes, and birds eating hair out of the grass.

Finally, Henry Jr. was speaking my language. Could I convince my family to let me do it?

CHAPTER 23
Off to Work?

At dinner the next night after choir practice, I told my family about the details of Henry Jr.'s job offer.

My mom gave me a blank stare, her fork of greens paused in the air near her mouth.

"J.D., I don't know . . . can we talk about this later? That seems like a bit much," she said.

I shot a hopeful look over to my grandmother to see if she would support me. Mom took a lot of her parenting cues from Grandma and Granddad.

"Veronica, I don't know if it's a good idea for J.D. to be down there getting in grown folks' business," Grandma said.

Not the answer I hoped for!

"Yeah, J.D., who is going to take you back and forth to Henry's!" Vanessa added.

"I have my bike, Vanessa."

Why did she have to butt in?

My last chance for support was Granddad. If he said no, it would be three against one and I definitely couldn't do it.

The next afternoon, instead of going to Jordan's house, I went home to try and catch my granddad before he started his burial insurance meetings at three o'clock.

I snuck up on him in his armchair and hugged him from behind like I always did when he was alone watching *The Young and the Restless*.

"That Victor Newman is still so smooth," I heard him say to himself.

"Granddad, I really want to go cut hair at Henry Jr.'s. I'm good at it! This way I won't even need an allowance." I made my case all in one breath.

At his core, Granddad was a businessman. He had been the boss at JCPenney and now he was his own boss.

"I will be like you," I said. "A working man!"

A smile spread across Granddad's face. He didn't make a sound for a long while.

"Okay," he finally said. "I will encourage your mom to let you try it, but just don't forget where

you come from. Don't embarrass me or your family when you are there!"

So that's how I became Hart and Son's first non-family employee.

The night before my first day at Hart and Son, I packed all the essentials: my video game console, my jar of candy, and a set of photographs of current hairstyles to put up on Henry Jr.'s wall. I didn't exactly know who'd come in for a cut or what it would be like to work beside Henry Jr., but I was about to find out.

CHAPTER 24
My New Competitor

The only thing I didn't like about my first day at Hart and Son was that it felt like work. There were adults around, so we kids had to be respectful and not goof off so much. I couldn't take breaks to play my own video games. And forget about turning on cartoons!

My feet hurt so much worse than anything I had ever felt after football practice.

I couldn't wait to sleep.

But all the money I made put me in a good mood. I cut ten kids' hair at seven fifty a pop and made eleven dollars in tips.

10 kids x $7.50 = $75.00

$75.00 + $11.00 in tips = $86.00

I was good at what I did, and my cuts were making kids all over the neighborhood feel good about themselves. What could be better? There was one kid who had come in because his mom gave him a bad haircut, just like I'd had, and he was so happy when he left.

As I walked up to the back porch, it looked like the lights were on in my room.

Everyone in Meridian kept their doors unlocked. We were all polite enough to never just walk into someone's house without asking!

Was I being robbed?

I tiptoed up to my door and heard the sound of a bunch of giggling girls.

I turned the knob and saw the last thing I'd expect: Vanessa and a group of her friends had taken over my bedroom!

There were hot curlers, bobby pins, gel, brushes, and a big ol' hair dryer with a bonnet. I even saw nail polish out, something Mom never let Vanessa wear.

Where'd she get that?

Jessyka was sitting in MY chair that I'd been using for haircuts and Vanessa had twisted her hair so she looked like a grown-up warrior.

"Hey, J.D.!" Jessyka said. "Guess what? My mom

said you could give me bangs. Are you up for the challenge?" she asked.

A grin spread all the way across Vanessa's face as she turned to me.

"Well, J.D., since you're out working on Saturdays, I thought I'd try doing my own thing in here. Kids' track-and-field is over until spring. You know I'm good at doing hair. Plus, Mom said it was okay."

MY room, MY setup, and MY chair?

Why did she have to copy me . . . didn't I have the idea to do hair first?!

"By the way, why did you decide to go work at Henry's?" Vanessa asked. "You could work with me and we could keep ALL our money in the family."

Working with my sister? That didn't sound like the best idea.

We were really different.

The last project we worked on together was the Sunday School Bake Sale, and we argued over whether to make cookies or cupcakes. We ended up putting both in the oven at the same time and burned everything to a crisp. Mom was super

GO!!
J.D.

annoyed that she had to take us to the grocery store to buy ready-made sweets.

Now Vanessa wanted us to do hair together? She would have every girl in the city in my room!

I had gone from teased to the best kids' barber this side of the Mississippi. Henry Jr. had tried to shut me down—even my clippers stopped working during the competition—and that didn't stop me, either! Did I need to help HER with her dream, too?

But one thing I knew about Vanessa is that once she got an idea stuck in her head, she never let it go.

I knew this wasn't over!

Acknowledgments

Thanks to: Michael for bringing my first concept to life; Akeem S. Roberts for doing an amazing job with the art; Joanna Cárdenas, and the Kokila Team; and last but not least, to Christina Morgan for making me go more in depth to create an amazing book. Thank you!